THE SAINT AND THE ROBOT

Gary Every

The Saint and the Robot
by Gary Every

All rights reserved. No part of this book may be reproduced or transmitted in any form or by any means, electronic or mechanical, including photocopying or recording or by any information storage and retrieval systems, without expressed written consent of the author and/or artists.

The Saint and the Robot is a work of fiction. Names, characters, places, and incidents are products of the author's imagination. Any resemblance to actual events or persons, living or dead, is entirely coincidental.

Story copyright owned by Gary Every

Cover illustration "The Saint and the Robot" and cover design by Marcia A. Borell

First Printing, May 2024

Hiraeth Publishing
P.O. Box 1248
Tularosa, NM 88352
e-mail: hiraethsubs@yahoo.com

Visit www.hiraethsffh.com for science fiction, fantasy, dark fiction, and more. Support the small, independent press...

The Saint and the Robot
Gary Every

On a moonless midnight, inside the world's greatest library, medieval Europe's greatest mind was hard at work. The keeper of the keys knew which student was awake, burning the midnight oil. He shrugged his shoulders and sighed. "Young Thomas."

The keeper of the keys walked between the long rows of books. It had been the same journey every night for years. The same doors, the same keys, the same hallways for decades. As a young man, the keeper of the keys had pondered the mysteries of the universe. Now he just walked and whistled. The head bishop stood in the center of the hallway and called to the keeper of the keys.

The bishop said. "It is time."

Together, they climbed the steep winding staircase. Their footsteps echoed but Thomas was so intent on his studies that he never heard them. When the head bishop stood in the doorway and cleared his throat, Thomas dropped his pen. As the feathered writing instrument fell, he tried to catch it and knocked a book from the table. Thomas spun around to catch the book and spilled a candle. The candle fell to the floor, bounced three times and landed on the book. Before the flame could flicker twice, the head bishop flew across the room and snuffed it out.

"Young Thomas," the bishop admonished, "We must be careful with fire, it is important to all mankind that the disaster of Alexandria never be repeated."

"Y-y-yes sir," Thomas stammered.

Thomas Aquinas was fourteen years old and his appetite for learning was never sated. He learned so fast, mathematics, astronomy, and so many languages. He was the most brilliant student the library had ever seen.

The bishop said, "The time has come for you to be expelled."

Thomas begged. "I am sorry about the candle."

The bishop explained. "There is a limit to what you can learn here. If this is truly to be the best library in the world, then I am afraid that her most brilliant student must go out and learn from others."

Thomas tried to protest but the bishop silenced him with his finger.

"It has already been discussed and decided," the bishop said.

The thought of leaving all these beautiful books, left an ache so deep that when Thomas touched his hand to his chest he expected to find a hole. Thomas stood at the front gate, preparing to walk out into a world he had never seen when the keeper of the keys interrupted. He whispered. "Over here."

Thomas Aquinas followed. The keeper of the keys wandered the labyrinth of hallways, taking the young lad deeper and deeper underground. Thomas wondered how this would help him to be expelled. Perhaps the keeper of the keys meant to hide him in the darkest basements the library had to offer. Thomas could hide for years, scavenging for bread crumbs. Thomas would read and read until his beard was long and white. The thought left Thomas deliriously happy.

The keeper of the keys turned a lock, and swung open a door, "This is my room."

It never occurred to young Thomas that just as the keeper of the keys walked the castle at midnight when the other residents slept, so too he must sleep while the others worked during the day. It was a simple room with a cot, table, fireplace and kettle. There were several shelves of books. Like a moth to a flame, Thomas was drawn to the books. "I have never heard of any of these." young Thomas exclaimed.

"That is because the bishop has banned them."

"Banned?!" Thomas said. "But why?"

"Because they do not glorify the Christian God." the keeper of the keys sighed. "I hide them so the bishop will not burn them."

Thomas gasped.

The keeper of the keys continued, "Still they are wonderful books. The collected works of the Archpoet are here, Greek philosophers, Roman encyclopedias, the journals of Arab explorers, and of course many volumes of alchemy."

"Alchemy?" Thomas reached out to pull a book from the shelves but the keeper of the keys slapped his hand.

"I did not bring you here," the keeper of the keys said, "To begin new studies on the day you are to leave."

"Then why did you ask me here?"

"To give you these," he pointed to a small pile of books on the table.

"But I have already read these," Thomas said.

"They are not for reading, they are for selling. You will need money to survive." and he hugged his favorite student.

Thomas walked out the castle door, stepping into bright sunlight. He had never seen the castle from the outside. It appeared quite big at first but as he walked away it shrank quickly until it disappeared from the horizon altogether. Thomas searched for bookstores.

The perfumes made his head swim. Thomas swiveled his head from side to side, staring at the beautiful young women. They wore silks and laces, gloves and stockings. Beautiful whores lined the streets, trumpeting strumpets advertising their services. Thomas had read about brothels in the library. They were always described as horrible places. This wasn't like that. The flirtatious eyes of the prostitutes were so different from the nuns. One curly haired girl touched his arm and offered him a glass of wine. It was his first taste of alcohol, wonderful and intoxicating.

In the morning when he awoke, Thomas was a little wiser in the ways of the world, a little wiser but not much. He was certainly poorer. Mary arose and put on her tattered tart clothing. She stood on the nearest street corner, waiting for her next lover. Thomas experienced his first broken heart, learning things which are not taught in libraries. Thomas walked fast, ignoring the raucous laughter of the taverns. The beggars begged in futility. Fortune tellers flipped their Tarot cards and offered to tell Thomas where he would find love but love was the last thing he was looking for. Thomas eventually came to a bookstore.

Thomas walked up and down the long narrow corridors, shelves stretching to the ceiling, stocked full with books. Thomas explored the uppermost shelves, climbing a rickety ladder where the most ancient, most expensive books were located. He discovered a book about a kingdom called Xanadu, an island filled with wonderful gardens.

"Finding what you need young man?" the shopkeeper inquired politely.

"There is no place to sit and read," Thomas said.

"If you want to read," the shopkeeper said. "Buy the book and take it home."

The bookstore owner was a bit of a drunkard. If Thomas got there early enough in the morning, the shopkeeper was too weary to chase him from the store. It gave Thomas a chance to read. Thomas read day after day. One day he heard a familiar voice.

"Thomas" Mary, the curly haired prostitute, ran up and hugged him.

Thomas's broken heart was just now mending. He was about to protest when his nostrils caught the scent of her intoxicating perfume. He hugged her back, squeezing her tightly.

"Oh Thomas," she sobbed. "Kiss me."

Thomas Aquinas, future saint, kissed the harlot in the middle of the crowded street, until their lips twisted like octopus limbs intertwined in a boiling ocean.

"Oh Thomas" she said. "Let us go get a bottle of wine and kiss some more"

When she said "Let us go get a bottle of wine," she meant of course that Thomas should pay for it and what good is wine without a little bit of bread and cheese. Why only whet the appetite when an entire dinner would be so much nicer. Thomas held her close. Mary told him her tale of woe. She had a son, a beautiful bright little boy. Determined not to raise her son in a brothel, she placed him in an orphanage where he would be brought up by priests and nuns who would make sure that he grew up right. She asked Thomas. "You can write, can't you? I knew you could, you look smart. I need you to write a letter."

Thomas sat at the desk, pen in hand, writing the letter as fast as she could dictate.

"It is his birthday," she said.

Tears welled up in his eyes. He could not help but wonder what circumstances led to him being left at the monastery doorstep or why his own mother did not write him a letter every year on his birthday. When Thomas was finished he gave Mary enough money to buy the lad a birthday present. Thomas awoke in the morning and she was already gone, in her place an unholy hangover had come to lie in bed beside him. With a heavy sigh, (and a throbbing headache) Thomas picked up his pile of books and went to sell them.

The bookstore owner chuckled. "What a relief it is to see someone more miserable than myself. That so rarely happens."

Thomas stepped forward, slightly wobbly, and placed his books on the counter. "I would like to sell these," he said.

The store owner laughed so loud that it hurt Thomas' headache. "All those times," the shopkeeper said, "You came into this store, hiding in the corners while you read, and you never bought a single thing. Now you expect ME to give YOU money."

A new customer entered the store. He was a tall bald man wearing a long plush luxuriant coat. The coat had several pockets and every pocket held some sort of device with levers, dials, and lenses for magnifying and telescoping. A beautiful red-headed girl held the door open for the stranger. What a beautiful young woman, long cascading red hair, freckles as soft as the spots of a fawn, and eyes blue like the arctic sky. She may have been the most beautiful girl Thomas had ever seen.

The shopkeeper bowed so low to the man he was practically kneeling. The tall bald man barely acknowledged the shopkeeper's existence, strolling between the shelves, looking slowly from side to side as if absorbing all the book titles at once. The beautiful girl held the door open for her mother. You could tell it was her mother as soon as she entered. She was long and lean, with a slight swivel to her stride which made you watch her hips as she walked. She was definitely the mother of this daughter. Two sisters followed inside, exact replicas of the first daughter. The shopkeeper shoved Thomas out of the way, sending him sprawling. The tall bald man was intensely skimming book titles, searching for something specific.

"Can I help you find something?" The shopkeeper approached, hands clasped together like pleading prayers.

The man asked. "Do you have any books about Xanadu?"

The shopkeeper shrugged.

Thomas pointed, "Up there."

"Where?" the tall man asked softly

Thomas pointed again, "Top shelf not far from the corner."

A red-headed daughter climbed the rickety ladder to retrieve the book about Xanadu. A second daughter helped Thomas from the floor. The third daughter handed the shopkeeper enough gold coins to purchase the Xanadu book. The tall bald man turned to greet Thomas. "My name," he said "Is Albertus Magnus."

"Pleased to meet you" Thomas replied

"Albertus Magnus is the greatest

alchemist who ever lived" the shopkeeper elbowed Thomas. "Everybody knows that. What kind of cave were you raised in?"

"Actually," Thomas replied. "I was raised in a monastery library."

"Interesting." Albertus Magnus said. "And you are?"

The shopkeeper stuck out his hand "Bert Snerdley, proprietor and owner of..."

Albertus Magnus ignored him. "I was talking to the young man."

"T-t-Thomas," he stammered. "Thomas Aquinas." Thomas blushed while the beautiful daughters brushed the dust from his clothing.

"Master Aquinas," Albertus Magnus asked, "Have you read this book about Xanadu?"

"That is the problem," the shopkeeper blurted out. "He is always reading books and never buying them."

"There is nothing wrong with a thirst for knowledge," Albertus Magnus said.

"Beautiful words sir," Thomas sighed. "Poems about butterflies and gardens."

"Gardening," the wife exclaimed, "I love to garden."

Albertus Magnus called to one of his daughters. "Open your purse and reward Master Aquinas."

"I cannot take your money sir," Thomas said.

"Can't take his money, foolish boy!" The shopkeeper was turning red in the face.

The great man's wife leaned forward and

whispered in his ear. Albertus Magnus laughed and clapped his hands together. "That is a wonderful idea." He announced, "My wife has proposed we accept your services in exchange for tuition at the next semester of my university. Welcome to school young man."

The shopkeeper blurted out, "But tuition is a thousand gold pieces."

Galatea Magnus answered, "We get enough coin from the dukes, princes, and royal astronomers. It will be nice to have a handsome young student on the estate."

Her daughters giggled.

Albertus Magnus said, "First day of classes are on the winter solstice."

Thomas answered. "I do not have a calendar."

Albertus Magnus reached into one his pockets and tossed an astronomical measuring device with gears and dials to his newest student. "If you cannot figure out the winter solstice with this, then you do not deserve to attend my university."

The world's greatest alchemist and his family walked from the bookstore.

The shopkeeper bought Thomas' books after all, eager to cultivate the friendship of the Albertus Magnus. Thomas went running down the street to find Mary. Perhaps she would consider moving to the university with him. His feet skidded to a stop on the cobblestone street. Mary was tenderly touching a finely dressed man wearing brand new clothes. He was an extremely ugly man, unkempt and loathsome, a knife scar on his cheek and meanness shining out from his eyes. Mary adjusted the rogue's cape, tying it tightly around his shoulders as it draped down his back like a brightly colored tapestry. She placed a silk cap atop his head and kissed him on the tip of his nose.

Mary said, "I feel guilty, sweet Thomas gave me money to buy my son a birthday present."

The ugly man guffawed, "Imagine a tart like you a mother with a son."

She replied, "But I do have a sun, you are my sun shedding light on my darkest days."

He grabbed her in his arms and held her tightly, "You have it wrong, wench. You are my sun and I am your earth and you shall be forced to orbit me for all eternity."

They kissed so passionately that his cap tumbled off his head to the cobblestones. Thomas turned before she could see him.

Thomas stared through the lenses and turned the dials of the device the great alchemist had given him. He shivered in the cold, calculating and measuring the stars. It was an extremely complicated device but as he observed, adjusting and calibrating, Thomas was amazed at what an incredibly precise instrument he was holding in his hands. He could not wait to bring it back to the library. At last, the stars revealed that the solstice was approaching. It was time for Thomas to board a stagecoach

The stagecoach jostled along the road before suddenly screeching to a halt. The door swung open and new passengers climbed inside. Thomas made room for the new arrivals. The passengers climbed inside the coach one after another while heavy luggage was loaded on the roof, thud after thud. The passengers kept climbing inside until Thomas was scrunched up against the window. The bench across from Thomas remained empty until the very last passenger stepped inside. The last passenger stretched out luxuriously as Thomas and five others crowded together on the opposite bench.

The man sitting alone was dressed in silks and jewels, asking, "Has anybody inquired of our fellow passenger's name?"

"Thomas," he answered, "Thomas Aquinas," and stuck out his hand.

The finely dressed man stared at Thomas' hand as if it were infected. "Duke Dracon" he said, not offering his hand in return.

Thomas turned his attention to the large man seated beside him, the one squishing him up against the wall of the coach. "And you are?" He inquired.

"His name is not important." The Duke said. "He is merely a servant."

"Where are you headed?" Thomas asked the Duke.

"To the university of the great Albertus Magnus."

"Myself as well." Thomas smiled.

"Are you a squire for your master?"

"I am a free man." Thomas said. "Albertus Magnus invited me."

"How charming," the Duke sneered between clenched teeth.

Classes began on the morning of the winter solstice. The snow was deep and the temperature was cold. Thomas' fellow students may have all been bluebloods by birth but standing in the knee-deep snow, they all turned blue on the outside as well. Thomas shivered. Thomas and his fellow students stood unable to speak because their teeth were chattering, waiting for their master to arrive. The world's greatest alchemist appeared at last wearing nothing more than a thin shirt and pants. no jacket, coat, cap, or gloves. Albertus Magnus did not shiver, not even when the wind gusted. He spoke his first words of the semester, "Let us begin with a courtyard feast."

The students stared at the tables in the courtyard, the tops covered with two feet of snow. Albertus Magnus clapped his hands and the snow began to melt. Galatea turned her head and called into the house. All three of her identical daughters came bustling out of the doorway, holding plates, tablecloths, and silverware. Working in synchronicity, the three red-headed girls swirled and twirled about the table almost as if they were dancing.

The snow began to melt far faster than was physically possible. The snow didn't melt really, it disappeared bit by bit without leaving behind a single drop of water to muddy the earth. Albertus Magnus clapped his hands again and plants began to sprout from the soil. Tiny stalks wriggled upward from the dirt, leaves leaping their sides, flowers opening into blossoms within minutes. As quickly as the snow dropped from the branches of the trees, leaves appeared, and almost instantly the trees were heavily laden with apples. The first bird to appear was a bluebird, followed by a bright red cardinal who warbled joyously in the treetops. Chickadees, towhees, and sparrows flocked to the growing greenery.

The red-headed daughters spread a feast upon the table, venison, baked ham, roast swan, ale and wine. There were exactly enough seats. Thomas was one of the last to sit, pulling up a seat beside Duke Dracon. The Duke harrumphed loudly.

"Is something the matter?" Albertus Magnus inquired.

"I am not," the Duke sneered, "used to sitting beside a commoner."

Albertus Magnus replied, "You are both students at my university."

"He smells bad." The Duke sniffed.

"We can fix your problem immediately," Albertus Magnus said. "Guards!"

Four large and surly looking guards arrived at the table awaiting instructions.

Albertus Magnus said, "Expel the Duke."

Duke Dracon protested, "You can't, I just paid you a thousand gold pieces."

"I can and I will," Albertus Magnus turned towards the guards, "Expel him immediately, this conversation bores me."

"But..." the duke started to say

One of the guards punched Duke Dracon so hard that all the air rushed out. While the Duke gasped for breath, the guards dragged him through the courtyard.

Albertus Magnus stood to deliver the first lecture of the semester. "The path to immortality is hard and only a few will find it."

Thomas wondered, was he here to discover immortality?

Albertus Magnus continued. "Most await the great day when the wheels of the universe shall be stopped and the immortal sparks shall escape from the sheaths of substance. Woe unto those who wait, for they must return again, unconscious and unknowing, to the seed ground of the stars, and await a new beginning..."

When the lecture ended, the feast began. Never had such a lavish feast been laid out before Thomas. He chewed and chewed, gristle and small bones flying from his lips and fingertips. If Thomas' table manners were enthusiastically bad it was nothing compared to the eager gluttony of the princes and noblemen seated beside him. Albertus Magnus ate slowly and steadily, not especially in a hurry to consume great quantities. His wife and three daughters did not eat at all.

"More wine sir," asked one of the beautiful daughters, standing beside Thomas with a pitcher in her hand.

Thomas said, "The stuff makes my head

swim."

"And when my lord goes swimming," she asked, "Does he wear a bathing suit or his birthday suit?"

Thomas blushed.

Galatea picked up a lute and strummed. Her long delicate fingers started an intricate melody. Thomas' brilliant mind was able to pick up immediately that the music represented a division of notes into mathematical sequences. Aquinas smiled, it had never occurred to him that there was a relationship between mathematics and music. The melody was precise. The three red-headed daughters clasped hands above their heads and danced. Three sisters swirled, moving together almost as if they were telepathic. They stomped and shuffled in perfect synchronicity. Mrs. Magnus' began to play faster and faster her fingers racing up and down the strings in a blur, fingers moving quicker than was humanly possible. Amazed, Thomas leaned back in his chair and watched her play, trying to reconcile the sound of the intricate melody with the frenzied blur of her hands. His mathematical mind was caught up in the relationships between harmony and rhythm, Thomas closed his eyes and leaned his chair way back. A dancing sister collided with the chair and Thomas tumbled over. One by one the dancers fell over him. The music stopped.

Albertus Magnus glared, clapped his hands and walked inside. Winter returned. Mrs. Magnus packed the lute inside its case. The three sisters continued to dance, silent metronomes ticking inside their heads, waltzing from the courtyard through the castle doorway. The students excused themselves from the table one by one. The birds all flew from the treetops, scattering across the sky. The flowers withered and died as the snow reappeared on the ground. Thomas Aquinas, the young future saint, was left cold and alone, shivering in the snow.

Thomas was up late, studying ancient alchemy texts in the university library. Exactly at midnight all the clocks in the castle began to chime, ringing in unison. Clocks had only recently been introduced from China. Several different clocks ringing in several different rooms, chiming in unison. Excited, Thomas ran from room to room, looking at the clocks, amazed that anything could be so synchronized.

"Ouch," Thomas kicked a piece of furniture while running in the darkness.

8...9..10... The clocks rang.

Thomas ran to the next room, bumping something with his knee. Something wobbled from the tabletop and fell to the floor, shattering into a thousand pieces of glass. Thomas never even looked over his shoulder, following the chiming clocks. In the next room, where the embers still glowed in the fireplace, the largest clock of all awaited. Thomas rushed up to the giant grandfather clock, pendulum swinging steadily, back and forth, back and forth.

11...12.

The chimes stopped. Thomas pressed his ear to the glass, listening to the movement of the machine.

Tick Tock. Tick Tock.

Giggle, giggle. The red-headed daughters scampered through the castle like scurrying mice. A candle appeared at the far end of the hallway, approaching Thomas steadily. "Hello Master Thomas," Galatea said. "Could not sleep?"

"Did not want to sleep," Thomas yawned.

She replied, "A young man needs his rest."

"Not when there is so much to learn." Thomas said. "I must study."

Mrs. Magnus said, "Learning is important, very important but dreaming more so."

"When you dream," Thomas asked, "What do you dream about?"

She sighed, "I can't say that I can recall ever having dreamed."

Tick Tock Tick Tock

"Is this clock from China like the others?" Thomas asked.

Galatea said, "This clock was built by my husband. He is quite handy at building machines. Amazing, if I do say so myself"

In a distant part of the castle a clock began to chime, Dong, dong, dong, beginning the long climb towards 12 and completely out of time with every other clock in the castle.

"Oh no," Galatea said, "That will never do. My husband will need to fix it."

Thomas said, "I want to learn how to build clocks. I want to know how they were invented and why. I want to know everything."

"Then you should ask my husband," she said.

Thomas awoke before any of the other students but not before the three red-headed sisters. Already, the pitter patter of their delicate feet could be heard. Albertus Magnus was at the far end of the castle, repairing the out of time clock. When Thomas walked into the room a large amount of machinery was scattered across the floor. The great alchemist laid out the parts in an organized fashion, tiny gears and springs stretched across the flagstone in the order they had been removed. Albertus Magnus muttered under his breath. "Hand me that screwdriver, will you?" the great alchemist asked.

"This one?" Thomas held the tiny tool in his hands. He had never seen anything so small.

"Yes that one," Albertus Magnus snapped, "Stop staring at it and hand it to me."

Albertus Magnus stuck an eyepiece up to his right socket and squinted through the lens while using the tiny screwdriver to deftly adjust a gear.

Thomas Aquinas asked, "Is it really so important that all the clocks be synchronized. I mean why is the exact time so important."

Albertus answered. "Time is what gives us history and if we do not accurately understand history how can we possibly imagine a perfect future."

Thomas asked, "Is it our responsibility to imagine a perfect future?"

"We imagine the future whether we take responsibility for it or not."

Albertus Magnus returned his attention to the clock. Some pieces went back inside the machinery and other pieces came out. Albertus Magnus handed Thomas a tiny gear, "Put this there." Thomas placed it carefully at the end of the row.

Albertus Magnus asked, "What do you know of the history of alchemy?"

Thomas shrugged.

Albertus Magnus continued. "For many years the ancient arts of alchemy were practiced on a Mediterranean island and a great civilization slowly arose, an amazing culture with incredible technology. Then an earthquake caused Atlantis to slide into the sea. Some of the survivors washed up on to the shores of Africa and soon the kingdoms of Egypt arose from the black fertile soil. There is much more to alchemy than turning lead into gold."

"Turning lead into gold?" Thomas asked. "Is such a thing possible?"

"A trivial act for trivial fools." Albertus replied.

There was a knocking on the door. A red-headed daughter rushed to greet the guest. After a brief conversation, the scurrying feet rushed towards Albertus Magnus. "Father," a beautiful daughter stated. "There is an angry man at the door."

"Let him in," Albertus Magnus said.

Duke Dracon stormed into the room, walking so fast that his jewelry rattled.

Thomas greeted him, "Duke how are you?"

"Silence!" Duke Dracon slapped Thomas in the face.

Albertus Magnus rolled his powerful shoulders, "What seems to be the problem?"

"You cannot expel me from your university on the first day of classes." the Duke declared.

"I can," Albertus Magnus replied. "And I already have."

"Then I demand my money back." The Duke screamed so loud spittle flew from his lips. "A thousand gold pieces is a lot of money."

"You were expelled for bad behavior." Albertus explained.

"You couldn't expect me to have dinner seated beside a servant boy!"

"I am not a servant boy," Thomas shouted, "I am a free man."

"Silence!" the Duke cried out, slapping Thomas hard. The Duke returned his attention to the alchemist. "A thousand gold pieces for what? What did I learn?"

Albertus Magnus replied calmly, "One would hope that you learned the lesson of not behaving like a jackass but judging from this conversation such is not the case."

Thomas chuckled.

The Duke went to slap him again but

Thomas responded first. Thomas picked up a book from the shelf, a good thick heavy volume, and went upside the Duke's head. Duke Dracon went down like a sack of potatoes. The three red-headed sisters dragged his limp body down the hall before tossing him out the castle door.

"If you want to learn how to build clocks then you will need this." and Albertus handed young Thomas Aquinas the eyepiece. Albertus Magnus exited just as all the clocks in the house began to chime the hour in perfect synchronicity.

Thomas flipped the eyepiece over and over between his fingers, amazed. Back at the monastery library the bishop had once described the infinite as that which was beyond the senses of man. This eyepiece allowed him to see things that were too tiny for the human eye, giving him a glimpse into the infinite. Thomas turned the eyepiece over and over between his fingers before putting it up to his eye. Everything was blurred. The disorienting vision made him dizzy, a wave of nausea washing over him. Thomas reached for the window to steady himself. Taking a deep breath of fresh air, Thomas glanced out the window and realized he was wearing the eyepiece backwards. Backwards, the eyepiece did not make small things appear larger but made distant things seem closer. With the eyepiece backwards, Thomas could look at the trees across the fields, observing the clumps of wildflowers growing at the base of the trunks. Thomas could see so clearly that he observed a butterfly feeding from flower to flower. The butterfly was beautiful.

Albertus Magnus took a tiny hammer and gently tapped a spring into place. Piece by piece, Albertus Magnus took the clock apart and put it back together beneath the watchful gaze of Thomas. Then Albertus Magnus took it apart again.

"Now you put it back together." Albertus said.

Then to his amazement, Thomas did. The incredible mind of the future saint had memorized every detail and his hands began to refashion the intricate machinery as if he had been doing it all his life. At the appropriate time it chimed in unison with all the other clocks in the castle. As the last chime sounded, Thomas asked, "What got you started studying alchemy?"

Albertus Magnus said. "It was many years ago when I was working as a scrivener in Paris. It was long and tedious work, copying entire manuscripts by hand. As soon as one book was finished you would start the next."

"I wonder if I ever read any of your manuscripts at the monastery library."

"Undoubtedly," Albertus Magnus replied proudly. "Working as a scrivener day after day was the same for years until one fateful afternoon when I stumbled upon an ancient manuscript bound in brass and written on papyrus leaves gilded with gold. The writing on the cover was in a strange tongue, unknown to me. There were the most amazing pictures inside, virgins being swallowed by serpents, flying unicorns, dragons who lived in caves beneath the sea, and images of something called the Philosophers Stone. I have dedicated my life to uncovering the secrets of the Philosophers Stone."

"But why," Thomas asked. "Why bother."

Albertus Magnus put down his clock making tools and looked Thomas in the eye. The great alchemist did not speak until he knew that he had his prize students full attention. Albertus Magnus said, "A soul that has gained no knowledge is blind, such a soul is tossed about among the passions which the body breeds; it carries the body as a burden. That is the vice of the soul. On the other hand the virtue of the soul is knowledge. He who has got knowledge is already divine."

"Amen," Thomas replied.

Thomas placed an ear to the face of the clock listening to the steady rhythm of tick tock, tick tock. "It is like a heartbeat," he said.

"The heartbeat of the universe," Albertus Magnus replied.

The breeze gusted softly through the open window. Thomas peered outside just as a butterfly fluttered by.

Thomas sat at the edge of the pond right when the sun was beginning to rise. The glorious colors of the sunrise reflected across the surface of the water like ripples. Thomas relaxed letting the morning wash over him. Thomas took a deep breath of fresh air and sneezed.

Ah-Choo!

With the sun climbing in the sky, the flowers began to open and Thomas sneezed from all the pollen. He picked one of the offending flowers, holding it in his hand. A butterfly fluttered by and drank the last drops of nectar from the dying blossom.

Splash.

A wave of water crashed over Thomas and the butterfly. Three red-headed sisters giggled.

"Hey boy," the girls teased. "Why don't you jump in and join us."

"You drowned him." Thomas said.

"Drowned who?"

One by one, the naked sisters climbed from the pond and stood beside Thomas to discover what he was holding in his hand. The wet girls dripped all over Thomas but he did not mind. God, they were so beautiful, perfect and flawless. One of the girls reached out to touch the wet butterfly. The blue wings flapped, fluttered, and then faded into stillness.

"Death is so sad," one red head said.

"And so unnecessary," said another.

Thomas recited what he had learned at the monastery, "Death is one of the punishments handed out when God banished Adam and Eve from the Garden of Eden."

The third sister plucked the butterfly from Thomas' hand and lobbed the dead insect into the air, hoping the wind might restart the wings. The butterfly fell back to earth like a falling leaf. The beautiful girl retrieved the dead butterfly and returned it to Thomas.

Thomas dropped the insect carcass to the ground, "Without the divine spark of life given to it by God it is not the same."

One of the sisters said. "Our father told us..."

The second sister said, "...The spark of life is indeed divine but..."

The third daughter finished "...It need not be provided by God."

Stunned by the heresy, Thomas placed his hands over his ears.

Suddenly all three girls turned their heads at once, staring fiercely back at the castle. "Mother is in danger!" They cried out as one. The three red-headed sisters threw on their clothes while Thomas stared at the distant castle, wondering how the girls could be so certain. The girls were off in a flash, fast as deer, leaving Thomas behind.

Thomas arrived at the castle as an angry crowd shouted out insults. Hundreds of townspeople had gathered at the castle door. They formed an unruly mob, each armed with the weapons of their trade, farmers with pitchforks, blacksmiths with hammers, coach drivers with whips, butchers with knives. Mary was in the crowd, looking bewildered and frightened. In the back of the mob, sitting atop his horse with a noose in his hands was the village hangman. Beside him, atop a slightly higher horse was Duke Dracon, a sneer crossing his face. His purse hung from his belt, laying slack against his hip, considerably lighter after he had used his coins to incite a lynch mob. The duke's goons were scattered throughout the crowd, hurling stones and curse words. The red-headed sisters were growling like feral cats. Galatea had been taken prisoner. Her hands were bound behind her back, her clothes torn and tattered.

From the back of the mob the hangman cried out, "Burn her, she is a witch."

The Duke laughed. One of his henchman stepped forward holding a torch. He lit Galatea's hair on fire. The hair went up in a puff of smoke, curling at the ends before disappearing in a little burst of flame, and for just a second, Mrs. Magnus was completely bald. Just as suddenly her hair grew back, strands writhing up from her scalp like thousands of tiny serpents emerging. In half a minute her hair had reached its familiar length. The crowd gasped.

"Burn her again," the hangman cried.

The Duke's goon smiled and lowered the torch. Thomas Aquinas screamed and charged. With all the ferocity he could muster Thomas rushed forward, determined to free Galatea from the unruly mob. The goon reached out his right fist and decked Thomas, flattening the young man onto his back. The three red-headed sisters howled and stepped forward with teeth bared.

"Silence!" cried out a stern voice. Albertus Magnus stood atop the parapets, his intense eyes glaring a fierce arctic blue. "Stop this nonsense at once."

The mob was stunned into silence.

"Burn her, she is a witch!" Duke Dracon spurred his horse and galloped away.

The sheriff repeated, "Burn her, she is a witch."

The goon with the torch stepped forward again, a lewd evil smile upon his face.

"Aaaarrgh!" Albertus Magnus clapped his hands above his head. A thunderbolt shot out from the blue sky, striking between the goon and the wizard's wife. The flash was so bright that it blinded Thomas for a moment. The boom of thunder was simultaneous, deafening everybody. The earth trembled violently, people fell to their knees. The castle tower shook, bricks crashing to the ground. The great alchemist held both hands above his head and chanted.

Storm clouds swirled, a tempest gathered. As fast as people could stand - the wind knocked them back to the ground. Albertus Magnus tilted his head back, eyes pointed directly to the raging storm. Albertus Magnus waved his arms in circles as funnel clouds dropped down from the sky, carrying off two members of the lynch mob. Large hailstones pelted the earth, striking stone and bone alike. The lynch mob melted away, racing beyond the edge of the storm. The red-headed daughters retrieved their stunned mother. As her daughters rushed her to the castle door, Galatea muttered, "Why do these humans hate me so?"

Albertus Magnus collapsed. The violent

storm disappeared as swiftly as it had begun. The alchemist lay atop the flagstone shivering, his eyes bluer than ice.

    Thomas was so focused on his curiosity that he had completely forgotten yesterday's danger. Thomas flailed and whirled, stumbled and stabbed, and sometimes succeeded in capturing a butterfly. Thomas was very careful not to hurt his floating captives. He would stare between his fingers where the butterfly was imprisoned, watching the wings slowly work, the antenna wiggle.
    Previously, Thomas had only learned by reading books, accumulating the knowledge of others. Now Thomas was learning by observing the natural world. All day long Thomas hunted the wide variety of butterflies feeding among the brightly colored flowers. Big butterflies, small butterflies, blue butterflies, spotted butterflies, all of them beautiful, all of them unique as jewels and each of them flying via the exact same mechanisms. Mechanisms, a funny name for insect parts, Thomas mused.
    In the distance, all the castle clocks began to chime at once, startling Thomas. He had been hunting butterflies all day without noticing he was slowly working his way back to the castle. As the clocks chimed in unison, Thomas could feel the beating wings of a captured butterfly stroking the inside of his hand. Suddenly Thomas had a new idea.

    Barons, princes, and various alchemical

apprentices wandered the halls looking slightly bewildered. Classes had been cancelled. There were rumors that Albertus Magnus had fallen gravely ill. None would speak of it. A few of the more industrious students gathered in the library. The royal astronomer spent the day in amorous pursuit of the red-headed sisters. The astronomer was rumored to have an extremely large telescope. A few students disappeared during the night, frightened away by the mob. One prince left because his kingdom had a military alliance with Duke Dracon.

Dinner was awkward. The red-headed sisters moved in synchronicity as they swirled around the table, hands full of platters, cups, and silverware, the pitter patter of their feet providing percussion. It was the only noise in the dining room. One of the red-headed sisters swooped in to refill Thomas' chalice. Thomas pointed to the empty chair at the head of the table and asked. "Where is your father?"

She replied. "He is exhausted."

A second sister brought Thomas a bowl of soup. She told him. "He caught cold from the storm yesterday."

Thomas suspected that Duke Dracon had instigated the lynch mob. Thomas could understand if they accused Albertus Magnus of being a witch, Albertus Magnus had powers that seemed beyond the reach of human understanding but why attack Galatea?

With lute in hand, Galatea said. "My husband wished for me to deliver tonight's lesson. This song is an example of harmony, movement, and the precise division of time, much like the heavenly bodies of astronomy."

She plucked the lute strings, slowly at first, giving each note a chance to resonate. Gradually but steadily, her fingers picked up the pace. The melody leapt quicker and quicker until her hands became a blur. Even at this frenetic pace the notes were divided evenly and rhythmically. Thomas closed his eyes and listened, trying to imagine the movements of astronomical bodies, stars dancing, planets turning, comets hurling, meteors hurtling through the sky. Her daughters danced to the music, touching only at the fingertips as they moved. The daughters danced, pirouetting, connected only by their giggles before coming together again, circling heel to toe, heel to toe.

Twang.

Mother missed a note. The offending string vibrated in off key discord. The daughters were so startled they tripped over each other, falling to the floor. Some surprised dinner guests spit out their drinks. Galatea sat there stunned, tears filling her eyes as she dropped the lute, running from the room. The red-headed daughters ran to comfort their distraught mother. Thomas stared at his food, his appetite had vanished.

The royal astronomer said. "She is a wonderful musician but everyone makes a mistake know and then. It just goes to prove she is only human."

Nervous laughter floated across the

dinner table.

Thomas flailed at the air as another butterfly escaped just beyond his grasp. Thomas tried again, stumbling and failing. The red-headed sisters giggled. They made capturing butterflies look easy. The sisters turned the hunt into a dance, leaping and waving their arms as if they had wings. One red-headed girl approached him with her hands clasped together and a tiny winged insect imprisoned inside. Thomas peered between her fingers, observing the fluttering butterfly.

All three sisters spoke in unison, "Master Thomas, have you learned what it is you wish to learn?"

"I have." he smiled.

"And what is that?" All three sisters asked in perfect harmony.

"Tick tock,' he laughed and ran towards the castle without explaining himself.

Bewildered the three sisters followed him, keeping pace easily, loping along and flapping their arms like giant butterflies, chasing each other.

Thomas discovered three seldom looked at clocks in remote parts of the castle. These clocks were important pieces of his plan. At least the parts of the clocks were important pieces of his plan. Thomas needed permission. Albertus Magnus was nowhere to be seen, had not been seen since the incident with the lynch mob. Thomas approached Galatea carefully.

Galatea was roaming the castle halls long after midnight. It was as if she never slept. Thomas approached and she reached out to touch him gently. With her hand pressed against his chest, Thomas could feel the rhythms of his own heart, beating steadily.

"Mrs. Magnus," He asked. "I was wondering if I could take apart the three clocks in the hat room, broom closet, and maids kitchen pantry. I believe your husband will enjoy my new project. I am going to build a..."

"Of course you can...." Mrs. Magnus said.

"Of course you can." She repeated.

Thomas was puzzled. He asked, "How is your husband?"

"Of course you can." Galatea said.

Galatea put her hand over her mouth but that did not stop her from speaking.

"Of course you can."

"Of course you can."

"Of course you can."

"Poor Mother," All three of her daughters spoke at once. Each stood at the entrance of a different hallway. Each daughter held a different clock, one from the hat room, broom closet and maids kitchen pantry.

"Of course you can."

The daughters rushed to their mother's side. Galatea kept staring straight ahead and repeating the same phrase. Feeling incredibly awkward Thomas picked up the clocks one by one and carried them back to his workshop Every time he returned, Mrs. Magnus was standing in the same place repeating the same phrase. "Of course you can."

Thomas stayed up till nearly sunrise, assembling the pieces of the clocks into his work of brilliant mad machinery. Thomas had just barely fallen asleep when there was a soft and gentle rapping at his door. Thomas opened the door and saw the three red-headed sisters standing there.

"We are heading into town," the one in the middle said.

"And thought you might like to accompany us," said the one on the right.

The sister on the left said, "We need someone strong to keep us safe."

Thomas stared into their beautiful blue eyes and could not refuse. The sisters insisted on visiting every merchant in the marketplace. They swirled scarves, tossed knives, and handled curious knick knacks before putting them back on entirely the wrong shelves. Thomas followed along trying to fix their wrongs but their were three of them. The sisters stopped at one tent where a craftsman manufactured mechanical parts. Thomas was delighted at this store, purchasing gears, springs and levers for his secret invention. The girls bought things too. They loaded up with bundles of machinery until their carrying basket was full.

"These will be perfect for mother," said one sister.

"These will be perfect for father, said the next.

The third sister explained, "These are for

a very important project - father is working on mother."

Next they stopped at a stall filled with exotic smells, strange roots and bizarre fruits. This shop was run by a tiny gnarled old woman. She had an owl perched on her shoulder. It was the owl who spoke.

"Who...who"

"We are the daughters of Albertus Magnus," the red-headed sisters said.

"Who?" the owl asked.

The three sisters pointed. "That is Thomas Aquinas,"

The owl flew across the room and perched atop Thomas' head. "He likes you," the old woman chuckled. The claws dug into his scalp, talons grasping clumps of hair.

"We are here," the three sisters spoke as one, "To purchase herbs for our father. He is quite ill, almost near death."

Near death? It was the first time Thomas heard anyone mention the famous sorcerer's condition so gravely.

"What is the matter? The old woman asked.

"He caught cold," said the first daughter

"More than just a little cold," said the second. "He is chilled to the bone."

The third continued, "He does not seem to be getting any warmer. If only he had a furnace instead of a heart."

"Do you have a piece of his clothing?" the old woman asked.

One of the sisters handed her a

nightshirt. The old woman sniffed the nightshirt and pressed it to her cheek. The hag's eyes rolled back in her head. The old woman trembled, and called to her owl in an unknown tongue. The bird flew about the room retrieving the things she requested.

"This ginger is from Cathay," she explained. "Ginger is good for almost every ailment. The Vikings in Iceland make a tea with this moss to keep themselves warm when the sun has disappeared for the winter. These are leaves from the sun drenched kingdoms of Prester John in Africa. These things will help your father but when one is dealing with alchemical ailments, there is no guarantee."

"Thank you, thank you," the daughters paid generously.

"Who?" the owl cried out.

A new customer entered the store. Thomas found himself staring at Mary. She apologized to the three sisters. "I am so sorry about the other day." She blurted out. "The Duke hired us to burn a witch and expel the devil himself from the castle. Then when we got there I saw that it was a family." Mary sighed. "How I wish I had a family, maybe I wouldn't be such a sinner."

"Me too," Thomas wondered again why he had been abandoned at the monastery.

"We'll be your family," the sisters hugged Thomas, causing the owl to fly off his head. Three red-headed sisters glared at Mary and stuck out their tongues.

The old woman said, "You still have not told me why you came sweetie?"

The curly haired girl blushed, "I seem to have picked up some sort of infection, a hazard of my profession."

The clocks in the castle all chimed the hour. The pieces of machinery in Thomas' hand began to rattle and ring. He had been working for hours and yet the metal in his hand was still more clock than magical machine. While the clocks chimed, his hands stuck inside the gears, a tiny hammer struck against his thumb.
"Ouch!" Thomas cried out, yanking his hand from between the gears. Thomas placed his thumb in his mouth. Thomas yanked his hand from the machinery so quickly that he stretched a tiny spring from corner to corner of the chassis. This fortunate accident gave the machine symmetry.
"Eureka!" Thomas shouted.
Furiously fast, Thomas turned screws, adjust levers, and tapped things into slightly different alignments. Thomas worked, thrilled with the inspiration of his invention. When the clocks in the castle began to chime next, the machinery in his hands did not respond.

Thomas rushed up the stairs eager to show Albertus Magnus his wonderful invention. The castle was silent except for the stomp of Thomas rushing up the spiral staircase. His steps echoed through the nearly empty castle. When Albertus Magnus did not emerge from his room for day after day the other students had left the castle one by one. After the red-headed sisters had refused every amorous advance of the persistent royal astronomer, he too had folded up his telescope and headed home. Thomas ran up the stairs, huffing and puffing, his invention in his hands.

"Ooof!"

Thomas tripped, his momentum stumbling forward. He raised his hands above his head, desperate to protect his prized invention. Thomas crashed SPLAT!, face first. Thomas bit through his lower lip and bloodied his nose. He took only a moment to check his machine for damage before resuming his race up the stairs, oblivious to his own injuries.

Thomas arrived at the top of the stairs and realized he had never been here before. He wondered if he was even allowed to be here. Thomas was so certain that Albertus Magnus would appreciate his invention, that he decided to knock. A red-headed sister opened the door. The first red head was followed by a second and then a third. From deep inside the room Galatea said, "Let Thomas enter.

Thomas held his invention before him, heading directly to the foot of the bed where the ill sorcerer lay. There were so many blankets piled high upon the bed, that Thomas wondered if the weight of all the fabric wasn't crushing the poor man. Albertus Magnus smiled weakly and sat up slightly. He looked very old, and tired. His body was the color of pond ice and he was shivering constantly.

Thomas presented his marvelous invention. "F-f-for you," he stammered.

The great wizard took the invention in his hands with great delight. "A jeweled butterfly," Albertus Magnus said. "How nice."

"Not a jeweled butterfly," Thomas corrected him, "A mechanical butterfly."

Albertus Magnus gasped as the iron butterfly flapped its wings. The butterfly slowly lifted from the wizard's palm and fluttered about the room. The red-headed sisters squealed with delight. The butterfly fluttered from floor to ceiling, a mechanical aeronautical insect acrobat.

"How amazing," Albertus Magnus clapped his hands together. "Incredible."

The red-headed daughters scurried about the room, trying to capture the mechanical butterfly. The young girls were fast and graceful but the mechanical butterfly fluttered just beyond their grasp, eluding capture. The sisters lunged at the butterfly at the exact same moment, their heads colliding with a loud thud.

Thomas tried not to laugh. Albertus Magnus let loose with a belly roar, guffawing like a braying mule. Galatea asked, "Perhaps you could show my daughters the best way to capture your elusive mechanical beast."

Thomas held out his hand and the magical mechanical butterfly floated across the room until it came to perch on the end of the future saints finger.

"How do you manage," Albertus Magnus asked, "To keep the butterfly balanced in the face of gusting breezes."

Thomas opened a trap door on the bottom of the insect allowing Albertus Magnus to glimpse inside. Albertus Magnus understood instantly. "The springs! Stretching the springs from corner to corner gives the machine balance and symmetry. It is a brilliant invention, how did you think of it?"

"By accident," Thomas confessed. "But once I noticed what it did, I stretched springs from here to here, there to there, here to there, and there to here."

"It is beautiful," Galeata Magnus said, "It flies almost as if it is dancing."

Albertus Magnus pushed away the stack of heavy blankets. He stood slowly on wobbly legs. The ancient wizard stepped away from the bed, "Your invention is brilliant Master Aquinas. You have given me some ideas." Albertus Magnus shuffled unsteadily towards his toolbox.

One of his daughters raced to his side, "Father you must rest."

"I have important work to do."

She guided him to a chair, "Drink some of the tea we made you, it has ginger."

"And Viking moss." said a second daughter.

The third daughter chimed in, "And leaves from the sun drenched kingdom of Prester John."

Albertus Magnus sighed, a long and heavy sigh, "All right, I will drink your tea, perhaps it will give me some extra strength before I begin my labors. If I need you Thomas I will call for you."

While Thomas slept, the butterfly hovered about the room, sailing gusts of snoring. The red-headed sisters burst into the room without bothering to knock. Thomas fumbled for his bedclothes. The sisters grabbed him by both hands and pulled him from bed. "Father needs you," the sisters said in unison and led him naked down the hallway.

The red-headed sisters pulled Thomas over the flagstone, so swiftly that he nearly stumbled. The mechanical butterfly flapped along behind. Thomas reached the door to Albertus Magnus' bedroom and while one red-headed girl threw open the door, the other two thrust the young man inside. The door closed behind and the sisters ran down the hall, too nervous to await the outcome. The butterfly hovered outside the closed door and waited.

Thomas found himself staring Albertus Magnus in the eye. Galatea lay on the bed. Albertus Magnus hunched over the opening in his wife's chest, delicate tools in each hand. He wore the desperate look of a cornered animal. The famous alchemist was performing surgery on his wife.

"Can I help?" Thomas asked.

"Yes!" Albertus Magnus pleaded.

Thomas stepped forward, hoping he was up to the task. He had read about surgery but had never actually attended an operation. Thomas hoped the sight of so much blood would not make him queasy. Coming closer, Thomas realized there was no blood, not on the sheets, not on the pillow, not even on Galatea. Staring between the alchemists hands, gazing deep inside the body of Galatea Magnus, Thomas saw nothing except gears and levers. The wife of Albertus Magnus was a machine.

Albertus Magnus said, "I was trying to stretch the springs like I saw on your butterfly machine but in my weakened condition I do not have enough strength."

Thomas hesitated, overwhelmed by the realization that Galatea was a robot. Laying sprawled on the bed, her skin slit open and the inner workings of her being on display, Galatea looked Thomas in the eyes and begged, "Please help me."

Albertus Magnus moved aside and Thomas stepped forward, sticking both his hands inside the open chest cavity of this woman he admired and loved. Galatea sighed and closed her eyes, trusting this future saint completely. Albertus Magnus watched intently, sweat breaking on his brow, terrified. Thomas stared at the complex inner workings of this human machine being in wonder.

Thomas reached deep inside the torso. As his fingers searched around he felt familiar things like gears, levers, and springs. He could pretend he was working on a machine and not a living human being. Thomas stuck his hand where the heart should have been and discovered a tiny piece of stone. This rock was vibrating slightly, humming. Thomas had found a piece of the Philosopher's Stone. Thomas forced himself to stick with business. He felt a spring stretch tight across the back of his hand. Thomas yanked his hand from the machine, the springs pinching his flesh as he pulled. The spring stretched, one end caught on a lever and the other on a gear.

"I never would have thought of that," Albertus Magnus said.

Neither did I," Thomas said. "The first time it happened was by accident."

"But then my boy," Albertus Magnus patted his apprentice on the shoulder, "You were smart enough to use it to your advantage."

Gears, levers, and springs, as long as Thomas focused on the parts and not the person he was able to work quickly and efficiently. Albertus Magnus handed him tools, making suggestions. Thomas took another look at Galeata's beating heart, the tiny chunk of the Philosopher's Stone. This was like no rock that Thomas had ever seen, wet and fluid, hard and yielding. Staring at it one could sense the sparks inside, a fire burning within. Thomas reached out to touch it.

As soon as Thomas made contact with her heart, Galeata Magnus gasped and sat upright. The Philosopher's Stone filled Thomas' head with visions. He heard the whip crack as slaves built the Egyptian pyramids. Images flashed of Druids dancing around the monoliths of Stonehenge, and elephants kneeling before a throne in the jungles of Cambodia. Thomas could not pull his hand from the Philosopher's Stone, visions flooding his brain. He saw terrible battles with tens of thousands of humans slaughtered by weapons yet to be invented. He saw wonderful flying machines and the horrors of death raining down from the sky. Thomas saw rocket ships carrying humans between the stars and he saw... The visions became too much and he fainted, falling to the floor. Thomas awoke with Albertus Magnus hovering over him, reviving him.

"That was amazing," Thomas said, "I have so many questions."

Albertus Magnus raised his hand, "There will be time for questions later, right now we must save the life of my wife."

The alchemist and his apprentice operated on Galatea deep into the night. At midnight, his hands buried deep inside the gears and levers of Galeata Magnus, all the clocks in the castle began chiming twelve times and for just a moment Thomas worried that Galeata Magnus might begin chiming as well. The moment passed and the two men continued, absorbed in their work. When they had sewn Galatea back together, she opened her eyes, sat up and hugged her husband. Albertus Magnus was so happy he cried. "Thank you so much young man for saving the life of the woman I love."

Thomas shook his mentor's hand and turned to leave. He stepped outside the door and discovered his mechanical butterfly hovering, waiting for him. Behind the closed door, Thomas heard a sound like a sack of potatoes falling to the floor.

"What was that?" Thomas asked.

"My husband has just collapsed from exhaustion." Galatea replied.

"Can I be of help?"

"I'll be fine," the alchemist answered in a weak trembling voice.

Thomas rushed to the door but realized it had been locked behind him.

Thomas slept all that day, through the night and late into the next morning. The mechanical butterfly hovered above the bed. There were also three chairs pulled alongside his dresser drawers. In each of the chairs a red-headed sister waited patiently for him to awaken. The three red-headed sisters thanked him for saving their mother and thanked him and thanked him and thanked him. Thomas fell back asleep, exhausted from all the thanking.

When he awakened again it was late afternoon. Thomas discovered the sisters were gone but the mechanical butterfly was still there. Thomas arose, yawned, stretched, and walked down the corridor, mechanical butterfly trailing behind, flapping its metal wings. Thomas walked out the front gate, over the drawbridge and towards the forest. The butterfly followed until they reached the meadow.

The flowers were collecting sunshine on a beautiful afternoon. There were birds perched in every tree. Countless butterflies hovered everywhere. Thomas released his invention, eager for it to make friends. As soon as his mechanical butterfly entered the meadow all the other winged insects flew away. The birds stopped singing and took to the sky. The flowers closed their petals as the mechanical butterfly flew past. The mechanical butterfly was content to follow Thomas. Thomas wondered if it was even possible for his invention feel happiness or loneliness.

When Thomas returned to the castle the three red-headed sisters were waiting.
"Father needs to speak with you immediately," said the first.
"Urgently," said the second. "There is no time to waste."
"This way," said the third and led him inside the castle.
The sisters walked rapidly as Thomas followed breathless. The sisters led him to the alchemist's bedroom and shoved Thomas inside. His mechanical butterfly followed.
"Welcome my boy," Albertus Magnus said from the bed, "Thank you for coming." Albertus Magnus looked pale and weak. Galatea sat beside him, comforting her husband.
"Thomas, come closer," the great alchemist used a finger to beckon. "I do not have the strength to speak loudly for long."
Thomas clasped his mentor's hand, his flesh as cold as ice.
Albertus Magnus stared into his apprentice's eyes. "The rigors of the operation have drained my strength. I am afraid I will not remain on this earth much longer."

"NO!" Thomas cried.

Galatea wept and kissed her husband tenderly on the forehead.

"You will recover," Thomas said, "If you drink the tea which your daughters prepared. You must rest."

Albertus Magnus replied. "You must listen closely as I tell you the last which I have to teach."

Thomas squeezed his hand.

"The beginnings of alchemy date back to when Adam and Eve were expelled from the Garden of Eden. As they were exiting the gates of paradise an angel took pity on the wretched couple and whispered the secrets of alchemy into their ears. The angel told them that if they ever mastered this mystical science then the gates of paradise would open once again. Of course Adam and Eve never succeeded."

"No one has," Thomas replied.

Albertus sputtered. "That is not true, there are some men who have unlocked the secrets of alchemy and opened the doors to eternity. My master was one of these."

"Who was your master?" Thomas asked.

"Hermes Trismesgastes," Albertus Magnus said. He is no longer visible to the human eye unless he chooses to be. He is no longer bound by the laws of time."

The castle clocks began to chime.

Albertus Magnus continued. "My master is a member of an elite religious order which keeps in contact with each other but not with humanity. Each of these sorcerers was allowed one apprentice, one student to whom the secrets of alchemical knowledge could be passed."

"You were one of those apprentices," Thomas half asked, half stated.

"I was," Albertus Magnus replied, "But apparently I will not attain immortality. I was distracted by my search for the Philosopher's Stone. I was young and arrogant, thought that I could break any rules, that any means were justified by my end."

"How did you find a piece of the Philosopher's Stone." Thomas asked.

Albertus said. "I do not wish to speak of such things. It was loathsome. I started in disreputable taverns and dark alleys and continued through catacombs and caverns until I found myself cutting deals with foul demons and misshapen fools on the edge of hell." Albertus Magnus sighed, "After those abuses of power, my master would not trust me with even the least of his secrets. Not able to pursue my studies in the way that I expected I followed new ideas, new avenues of exploration and invention. I became fascinated with machines and the way the Philosopher's Stone animated them, designing more and more intricate devices capable of more and more amazing possibilities."

He placed his hand on his wife's knee. "In a way I was able to open the gates of paradise anyhow." He stared deep into Galatea's eyes. "I discovered true love."

She kissed him.

Thomas said. "I am happy for both of

you."

Albertus Magnus said. "I am not immortal but now that we have fixed her Galatea is. Having experienced both extreme loneliness and true love I would never condemn Galatea to an eternity of being alone. She has so much to offer, loyalty and friendship. I would never have believed that a woman could be capable of such intense passion."

Galatea blushed.

Thomas had never seen her blush before. He wondered if it was possible for a machine to be embarrassed. Albertus Magnus coughed. He coughed and coughed spasms wracking his body. His wife held him tight, trying to ease his illness. Thomas was taken aback by the violence of the seizures. Albertus spoke to Thomas, his voice barely rising above a whisper.

"My boy, I am about to bestow upon you the most precious gift I have to offer. After my death I was hoping you would be Galatea's next husband. She will do her best to make you happy and all you have to do in return is show her kindness and consideration. I have spoken with Galatea about this and she approves. She has no desire to spend all eternity alone. When your days are nearly finished, you too will need to find a suitable mate for your wife. Are you willing to accept these responsibilities?"

"I do." Thomas replied.

"Interesting choice of words," Galatea giggled.

Thomas Aquinas and Galatea Magnus

both sat on the edge of the bed, one on each side of the dying alchemist, holding and comforting Albertus in his last moments. As his strength faded the two most important people in his life escorted Albertus Magnus to the afterworld, the fire in the hearth slowly burning until the last embers faded. Thomas gradually slipped into sleep. When Thomas awoke Albertus Magnus was dead. His wife sitting loyally beside him. The room was dark and cold.

"I am so sorry about your husband." Thomas said.

"I too am sad about the death of Albertus Magnus... my husband." and she placed her arms around Thomas' neck.

Galatea and Thomas inspected each other closely, staring deep into each others eyes. Thomas was hoping to see a glimpse of her soul, fearful of seeing gears and glass, but all he saw was his own reflection.

"I do." Galatea said, leaning forward to kiss Thomas.

It was like no kiss Thomas had ever felt before, warming his entire face. As their tongues twisted, Thomas could feel his heart beating rapidly. He wondered if hers was doing the same. Thomas placed his hand upon her breast, hoping to feel her beating heart and as his fingers pressed into her flesh he only felt gears spinning, tick tock, tick tock. How could Thomas marry a machine?! It was blasphemy.

"I do not." Thomas cried out, breaking the embrace.

He ran to the fireplace, grabbing a small

axe. With a mad gleam in his eyes Thomas marched towards his wife. "Heretical abomination!" he screamed.

Galatea raised her hands above her head. Thomas brought the axe down, the blade slicing through skin, revealing the levers and gears underneath. "Please! Do not kill me." Galatea begged. "I love you." She sobbed.

Enraged, Thomas brought the axe down again, severing an arm. Thomas knew from working on her pulleys, and springs that Galatea was much stronger than he was and could have stopped him at any moment. Yet, she chose not to. Instead she pleaded for her life, begging Thomas to spare her. She sobbed. "I am your wife."

Thomas swung the axe. "You are a diabolical infernal machine - a mechanical heresy." His next blow severed Galatea's head from her body. Consumed by his blood lust, Thomas killed her again and again.

"Oh Albertus," Galatea moaned while her battered torso crawled across the floor. She carried her head under her remaining arm. Galatea slowly traversed the flagstone until she came to rest against the body of her dead husband, placing her severed head upon the chest of Albertus Magnus, his heart no longer beating inside. Her eyes still open, Galatea cried.

The brutal attack reopened the wound from her surgery. Thomas dropped the axe and reached inside her, plucking the Philosopher's Stone from her chest. With the

Philosopher's Stone in his hand dreams of incredible wealth filled his head, visions of ruling over a vast empire, flooded his brain. What would Thomas do with unlimited magical powers? Thomas nearly swooned, recovered, screamed and threw the Philosopher's Stone into the hearth. The stone exploded, spreading fire across the room, the drapes and bed caught on fire. Galatea Magnus screamed and began to melt. The Philosopher's Stone swelled in size as it burned, doubling, tripling, quadrupling in size, burning with a white light too bright to look at it.

Thomas turned to flee, horrified by what he had just done. Aghast he watched flames consume Albertus and Galatea. Thomas ran down the spiral stairs, his mechanical butterfly following as the castle burned behind him. Thomas ran out the castle and over the drawbridge. The red-headed sisters shrieked in horror, "Father! Mother!" They wailed. Thomas continued running.

Thomas' feet pounded the road He gasped for air. His mechanical butterfly followed along effortlessly. Thomas left the castle further and further behind. The roar of galloping horses approached him. A herd of horses crested the hilltop, riders atop of each, racing towards the burning castle. The sheriff was leading a posse of thirty men. At the sight of Thomas, the sheriff stopped his horse.

"You there," the sheriff gestured at the burning castle, "What just happened?"

"Alchemy gone terribly astray." Thomas

sobbed.

"Like that." one of the deputies pointed at the butterfly hovering just above Thomas' shoulder.

"Yes," Thomas cried out, swinging his fists wildly. "Curse you, you infernal abomination," Thomas tried to hit the mechanical butterfly but the butterfly floated just beyond his grasp. The more he missed, the more enraged Thomas became. "Die heresy!" Thomas leapt at the butterfly.

The posse laughed hysterically.

"He's gone quite mad." the sheriff proclaimed spurred his horse and raced towards the burning castle. Thomas sat by the side of the road and sobbed. His invention hovering above his head just beyond his grasp. Thomas cried, listening while the galloping horse hooves raced away. The horse hooves receded into the distance, clouds of dark black smoke blotting the horizon. Just as the horses reached the castle the three red-headed sisters began wailing.

Thomas stopped sobbing, got up and ran, remembering that he was a murderer. Wasn't he? He had killed Galatea. Could a human being murder a machine? He could hear the sound of the posse leaving the castle, racing towards the village. Fearful of the gallows, Thomas tried to outrun the galloping horses. Then Thomas heard something much more frightening. In front of the horses and coming nearer with every step, was the sound of six pounding footsteps. The red-headed sisters were chasing him and Thomas needed somewhere to hide.

Drip.. drip... drip...drip
Cold water fell on Thomas' forehead. He dared not squirm or whimper.

"Which way did he go?" cried out a red-headed sister.

"I lost the trail" shouted the second.

"This way," called out the third sister, and ran down the hill calling his name. "Thoooomas!" All three red-headed sisters ran down the hill

Thomas waited for the sound of the footsteps to fade. A rat ran across his chest. Thomas squealed, flailing at the scampering rodent. Another drop of water fell on his head. It was such a miserable hiding place that no one, not even the red-headed sisters thought of looking in the basement of a windmill. The wind gusted, catching the sails and pushing the windmill arms. As the arms spun they turned a shaft which moved a millstone to grind against another large millstone. The groan of stone on stone echoed throughout the tiny basement.

Thomas spied some spilt grain on the floor. Who knows how long it had been sitting there but Thomas was ravenously hungry. He placed a kernel on his tongue and bit. The husk rattled his teeth. His empty stomach rumbled. Thomas gathered a handful of grain and placed it between the stones. The wind blew, pushing the windmill, grinding the millstones. Thomas reached out for a pinch of sweet nutritious food. The smell of freshly crushed grain attracted mice from every crevice. Rats ran up his pant legs. A rodent was caught between the moving stones emitting a sharp short squeak.

The wind now carried the smell of fresh blood. The basement filled with thumping and slithering sounds as predators crawled from the darkness. Thomas ran for the door. He hade no desire to discover who or what might be attracted to fresh blood in this cold dark place.

Thomas ran out the windmill door, bursting from the basement into the sunshine, his eyes blinking furiously. Out in the fresh air the wind carried all sorts of new scents to his nostrils. His ravenous hunger only made his sense of smell stronger. The sheriff was looking for him. The Duke's henchman might be looking for him and Thomas knew beyond the shadow of a doubt that the red-headed sisters were searching for him. Before he could hide, Thomas needed food. How could he hide if his stomach was rumbling? The wind gusted and carried the scent of apple pie.

Apple Pie! Thomas jumped for joy. Apples were exotic botanical technology which had arrived with the same explorers who had returned from China with the first clocks. Sweet delicious apples, it did not matter if they were red or green, the smell of the freshly baked apple pie made Thomas drool. Thomas followed his nostrils.

Thomas ran to the edge of a great estate.

Thomas scrambled over a wall and then snuck through an orchard. It was the largest apple orchard he had ever seen, tree after tree arranged in rows, all the branches hanging heavy with bright red fruit. He snuck through the grove quickly, coming to a giant mansion where an apple pie sat cooling on a ledge. Thomas motioned for his mechanical butterfly to remain in the orchard, hidden in the foliage.

Thomas approached the house cautiously, sneaking through the shrubbery. Thomas was reaching for the pie with both hands when he heard footsteps. Thomas ducked beneath the ledge. The footsteps strode straight to the open window. Thomas tried to shrink inside the shrubbery, wishing he could turn himself invisible. A pair of hands adjusted the pie where it sat on the ledge, while Thomas thought himself as small as he could possibly think. A knife cut through the crust and scooped a big chunk of pie onto a plate. The footsteps placed the pie piece on the table. Thomas reached up and scooped a finger full of apple pie from the open hole in the crust. He shoved his fingers into his mouth, cinnamon, clove and nutmeg drooling down his chin. The apple pie was so delicious and so HOT! Thomas clapped both hands over his mouth to stop himself from screaming. It burned the roof of his mouth but was so delicious. The person eating at the kitchen table chomped away in great big gulps, snuffling and snorting.

A second set of footsteps entered the kitchen, boots clicking against the flagstone. The second footsteps spoke in a voice belonging to the sheriff. "The castle has burned down. The wizard is dead and his mechanical concubine has been destroyed."

"Did you find the Philosophers Stone?" the Duke asked, mouth full of pie.

"We searched the castle ruins but did not find it."

"Did you search the dead?' the Duke asked.

"We searched the wizard but he did not have any magical stones."

"Did you search his wife?"

The sheriff replied, "She did not have it."

"Then the boy must have the Philosopher's Stone!" Duke Dracon exclaimed.

"Are you sure?' The sheriff asked

"The Philosopher's Stone would not just burn to ash," the Duke explained. "It is a magical stone. It is not of this world"

A butterfly wandered through the shrubbery, gliding on black and yellow wings as it floated between the leaves. Thomas tried not to stir as the butterfly approached.

"If the boy has the stone," the Duke said "Then we must find him and arrest him."

"Arrest him - on what charges?" The sheriff asked.

"Murder of course." the Duke said.

Thomas gulped.

"There is no evidence the wizard was murdered." the sheriff said.

"And his wife?" The Duke asked.

The sheriff replied, "She was battered with an axe but is it possible to murder a machine?"

The black and yellow butterfly landed on Thomas' nose. Thomas dared not move, dared not make a sound. The butterfly made his nose itch but Thomas dared not sneeze.

"It does not matter if he committed a crime," the Duke said, "You must arrest him. We can torture him until he confesses to whatever crime we choose and then torture him until he tells us where the Philosopher's Stone is. Then it does not matter if we kill him."

"I suppose not," the sheriff said.

"But we will kill him anyways." the Duke said.

The butterfly departed. The sheriff left. The Duke exited the room. Thomas licked the pie pan clean and fled, leaping the estate walls and running as fast as he could.

Knock. Knock. Knock.

It was the middle of the night and there was no answer. He knocked again. Knock. Knock. Knock.

The door swung open and a villainous rogue stood behind it, knife scars on his cheek and a candle in his hand. The rogue was unkempt, unshaven, but he was well dressed, attired in brightly colored silks. The rogue greeted Thomas brusquely.

"The brothel is closed." the rogue said.

Thomas blurted out, "I am here to see Mary."

"She is not working right now, she is sleeping." The rogue tried to close the door.

Thomas wedged his foot in the door jam.

"Please, I am a friend. I need to speak with her urgently."

The rogue put his shoulder to the door, crushing Thomas' toes. The rogue spit as he spoke. "Mary don't have any friends except me, she don't need any friend except me."

"Please," Thomas pleaded, refusing to pull his aching foot from the door.

"If you want to see her you will have to pay."

"Of course," Thomas agreed.

"At this time of night you have to pay double." The rogue said.

"...Certainly"

"Wait here." the rogue departed and was soon replaced by Mary.

"Hello," Thomas waved shyly.

"Oh Thomas," she smiled and threw her arms around him. At the back of the house a door slammed.

"Do not mind him," she said, "He is jealous." and then she kissed him. The power of her passion left him a little dazed.

"We must talk," Thomas blurted out, "I need somewhere to hide."

Thomas began to explain about Albertus Magnus and his robot wife. The curly haired prostitute listened with rapt attention. He spared her none of the details from the gradual death of Albertus Magnus to the brutal battering of Galatea, tears filling his eyes. Mary cried too. Thomas stammered as he described throwing the Philosopher's Stone into the hearth, the explosion that caused the castle to burn in flames. He told her he was hiding from the duke, the sheriff, the posse and the red-headed sisters. When Thomas finished she kissed him again. He kissed her back. Thomas closed his eyes, lost in her fragrance. The gallop of horses clattered on the cobblestone street, a large group of horses approaching quickly.

"You need somewhere to hide," and she flew across the room, opening a small closet, shoving Thomas inside. She had no sooner shut the closet when the front door of the brothel flew open wide. The rogue stepped inside, followed by Duke Dracon. The sheriff could be overheard shouting orders to the posse outside.

"We are here to collect the reward money," the rogue said.

"What reward money?" the curly haired prostitute asked.

"Your friend Thomas is a wanted man." the rogue said. "A very wanted man."

He has committed acts of murder," the Duke said.

"He has not." Mary defended him, shaking her head so hard her curls rattled

"I am afraid Thomas Aquinas is accused of murder," the Duke said, "And now he is pursued by the consequences."

"He is pursued by villains." she said.

"Where is he?" the rogue shouted, tossing furniture around the room. "Where is he?"

"He is not here," the curly haired girl said.

"Liar!" the rogue slapped her with the back of his hand.

The Duke asked, "Are you certain he was here?"

"I saw him with my own eyes," the rogue screamed, "And I am certain he is still here. That reward money is mine. I will beat it out of her."

"No need for that." the Duke said with a lewd smile. "You say the young lady is Thomas Aquinas' dearest friend in the whole wide world?"

"She is," the rogue said. "That is why I am so certain she is hiding him."

"Perhaps they are lovers?" the Duke inquired.

"If they are," the rogue said, "Then I will beat that habit out of her too."

The Duke said. "Maybe the trick is to bring him to us. I have always found the dark passions to be much stronger than the noble impulses. One of the darkest passions is jealousy. How many gold pieces for the chance to make love to the young woman?"

"Never!" she cried out angrily.

The rogue named a price.

"And how much to extend the opportunity to the entire posse?" The Duke counted out a large stack of gold coins.

"I will never kiss you," the curly haired prostitute stated.

The Duke slapped her, "I do not want you to kiss me. I do not want you to enjoy this." He slapped her again and again. "We will abuse you until you gladly tell us where Thomas Aquinas is hiding." The Duke spit on her.

Thomas leapt into the room and grabbed the Duke from behind. As Thomas clutched the Duke's back, his fingers found the thick gold chain of the Duke's necklace. Thomas pulled hard on the chain and cut off the Duke's windpipe. Mary screamed.

Standing outside the door, the sheriff laughed while a member of the posse shouted out, "Give her hell Duke, anybody can see she is a lying little tart."

Thomas twisted the chain tighter and tighter with both hands, closing the noose. Mary squirmed free of his grasp. The Duke clawed at the gold chain with his fingernails, trying to break the metallic bonds. The links dug deeper into his neck while Thomas twisted the chain. The Duke's face became red then blue, followed by purple as his lips foamed. He tried to scream but died silently. The Duke collapsed to the floor. The curly haired prostitute screamed.

The posse outside the door, hooted and hollered, eagerly waiting for the Duke to finish so they could take their turns. The rogue rushed to the dead body and removed the gold necklace. The rogue slipped the necklace over his own head, wearing it greedily.

"Oh Thomas what have you done?" Mary embraced him.

One by one the rogue pulled off the Duke's rings and stuffed them in his pockets. Then he ran out the front door screaming

"Murder! Murder! Murder!"

Thomas escaped out the back door just as the posse ran in the front. The sheriff went straight to where the Duke lay on the floor while the posse gathered round. He checked for a pulse or sign of breathing. "He's dead," the sheriff pronounced, "There is nothing more we can do here. Stop wasting time and chase that criminal!"

While the posse took off in pursuit of Thomas Aquinas, the sheriff remained behind and arrested Mary. Thomas ran and ran while the sheriff bound her in chains.

She cried as she climbed the steps of the scaffolding, slowly reaching the gallows deck. Her guards each held an arm, as they escorted her directly beneath the noose. The town was buzzing with gossip, the death of the wizard, the burning of the castle, the murder of the Duke. Most of the town and many of the countryside had come to watch the hanging. They were hanging a woman. Merchants and masons gawked. Clergy and innkeepers whispered back and forth. An ugly old woman tried to sell moldy potatoes. Children clung to their mothers skirts, afraid to watch the gruesome proceedings.

On the gallows platform, black hood on his head, the hangman said "Howdy Miss."

"Hello," Mary replied politely.

"Shame to end a pretty smile such as yours," the hangman said. "Thanks for the times you eased my loneliness."

Mary blushed. It was a familiar voice but she was unable to recognize the face beneath the black mask. Sometimes being a prostitute in a small town was awkward.

The ugly old woman selling potatoes moved slowly through the crowd. She was very ugly and the potatoes were very rotten. Step by step the sheriff climbed the scaffolding, his boots striking the stairs. The sheriff came to stand beside the executioner and addressed the crowd. "This young woman," he said, "Has been found guilty of murdering Duke Dracon. For this heinous crime she shall be hanged to death."

"She did not," cried out someone in the audience. Many in the crowd booed. "The Duke was a wanker." shouted out another. Mary heard a sniffling sound beside her. Looking at the hangman she saw tears dripping down his chin and falling out from under his black hood. "Forgive me" he wept as he slipped the noose around her neck.

She leaned over and kissed her executioner on the forehead.

The crowd cheered. The sheriff stepped back and the priest stepped forward, saying a prayer for the executed. For the first time Mary began to cry.

"Potatoes for sale," the old woman cried in a weird hideous screech "Potatoes for sale." She moved to the very front of the gallows, apparently oblivious to the high drama unfolding. No one bought any of her old moldy potatoes. The old woman wore a heavy cloak with a hood drawn over her face, which judging by her hideous screeching voice must have been ugly indeed. She was a hunchbacked old woman and those who stared closely could see the hump flutter from time to time.

The priest rambled on while the crowd grew restless. "She is innocent!" shouted someone in the rabble. The priest ignored them and continued his sermon. The sheriff leaned forward and whispered in the priests ear, "Hurry it up." Someone finally bought a potato. They threw it at the sheriff.

"Ouch" the sheriff shouted.

The duke's henchman stepped forward, menacing the crowd. The duke might be dead but as long as the money held out the posse was still loyal. Lots of people bought potatoes, spuds raining down on the stage. The henchmen stepped into the crowd swinging fists. More old moldy potatoes flew at the gallows. While the melee raged the priest continued with his overly long sermon. Suddenly the sheriff stepped forward and ended the prayer abruptly, "God Bless us All. Amen. - Now Hang Her!"

The old woman leapt up on the gallows, dropping the basket of potatoes, moldy spuds rolling everywhere. She threw off her cloak revealing the old woman was really Thomas Aquinas in disguise. As he threw the cloak from his head the mechanical butterfly escaped, hovering above him.

"You cannot hang her." Thomas declared loudly. "I murdered the duke."

The riot stopped instantly. Both villains

and citizens staring at Thomas. The sheriff responded first, stepping forward to arrest Thomas. Thomas had not thought this part through, concentrating solely on rescuing Mary. Thomas put up his fists, defending himself. The sheriff punched Thomas in the nose, flattening him on his back. The henchmen rushed the stage and surrounded the fallen future saint. Their blows rained down fast and furious, hitting and kicking. While the posse pounded Thomas, the sheriff went to hang Mary. As soon as the sheriff's hand reached for the trap door lever, a fist came flying from his blindside and knocked him backwards with a powerful punch.

"You cannot hang her," the executioner shouted as he shook his sore hand. "She is innocent."

Mary escaped during the confusion. The posse beat Thomas into submission and then beat him a little bit more. They dragged him to the gallows.

"Executioner," the sheriff shouted, "Looks like there will be a hanging after all."

The crowd cheered, their blood lust aroused. The hangman shrugged. He had no problems hanging a man who had confessed to murder. Thomas gulped as the hangman adjusted the knots. Thomas head was placed inside the noose, cord rubbing against his neck. The posse chuckled. The crowd waited breathlessly for the execution.

Suddenly feral yowls erupted from the edge of the plaza. Three female figures leapt with feline quickness, jumping and somersaulting up and over the crowd. The three red-headed sisters approached from different directions all six feet landing with a thud on the wooden gallows platform at exactly the same time. The sisters snarled, baring their fangs and extending their fingernails like claws. The henchmen backed up, slightly bewildered and extremely frightened.

"Release Thomas," the red-headed sisters demanded.

The hangman released him. It was only a job, so he did as the fierce sisters demanded. Thomas ran to the back of the gallows and leapt on to the back of a horse. Landing on the saddle awkwardly made Thomas wince but he wasted no time tapping his heels to the flanks, urging the horse to run away.

"That's my horse," the sheriff shouted.

The red haired sisters roared. There were hideous screams and the snap of breaking bones as the red-headed sisters slaughtered the posse and the sheriff. The crowd fled. Thomas urged the horse faster because he knew that when the red-headed sisters had finally disposed of the posse they would be coming after him.

The horse ran like hell. The frightened equine did not want to wear this unknown rider and did his best to lose him, scraping his side against fences, ducking beneath low hanging branches, leaping over bridges and chasms. Thomas hung on for dear life, terrified of letting go. Behind him Thomas could hear the red-headed sisters, six feet pounding the earth in unison like the beating of a war drum. No matter how fast the frightened horse ran, the red-headed sisters were quicker. The horse ran until his flanks were coated with foam. Thomas could hear the red-headed sisters breathing, lungs chugging steadily. The mechanical butterfly flapped his wings furiously, racing ahead of the galloping horse and urging him onwards. This noble horse did the best it could, running itself into exhaustion, and then it ran some more.

The horse ran to the edge of a cliff. The mechanical butterfly leapt out beyond the precipice, hovering in mid air waiting for horse and rider to follow. There was nowhere left to hide. The cliff was sheer and the river far beneath. A jump would leave him little chance of surviving. Thomas dismounted. The red-headed sisters approached like a pack of hunting lionesses, cutting off all avenues of escape. The red-headed sisters advanced to within ten feet and stood silently. For just a second the mechanical butterfly tried to hover between them, fluttering protectively. Thomas brushed it aside.

With tears in his eyes, Thomas apologized. "I am so sorry that I killed your mother. I was consumed by grief, rage and madness."

The three red-headed sisters cried too, tears streaming down their faces. "Oh Thomas," they sobbed "We forgive you."

"I thought you were following me" Thomas said "Because you were trying to kill me."

"We were following you," the first sister said.

"Because," said the second sister, "We are now orphans completely alone in this world and..."

The third finished "We would like to ask for your hand in marriage."

All three red-headed sisters dropped to one knee, extending a hand forward, clasping them together and offering Thomas a wedding band.

Thomas gasped.

"I cannot marry you for the same reason I could not marry your mother. A man cannot marry a machine."

"But we are only half machine," the sisters cried in unison. "The other half is human."

Thomas shuddered. "It is an unholy union."

"But we love you," said the first sister.

"And what is more holy than love." said the second sister.

"We will love you forever, for all eternity," said the third sister.

"No." He said, stifling a sob.

The red-headed sisters wailed in anguish. "We will not wander the earth alone, scorned by humankind for all time." The red-headed sisters said, "We will not spend out entire immortality cloaked in loneliness."

The red-headed sisters removed daggers from their belts and held them poised above their heads. Thomas cowered, certain of being stabbed. Instead, the red-headed sisters slit their own throats. Thomas screamed in anguish as blood and oil ran down the front of their dresses. One by one the red-headed sisters toppled over, sprawled dead across the top of the grass. Thomas fell to his knees and wept.

In the highest watchtower of the monastery library there was a candle burning. The keeper of the keys looked up, slightly startled. No one had been studying at this late hour in a long time. The keeper of the keys investigated, climbing the stairs one by one. The keeper of the keys huffed and puffed. He was a little older and a little fatter. He wandered the corridors late at night, every night, just as he had for years and now he was investigating the light burning in the highest watchtower, climbing one stair at a time. Even from far away, the keeper of the keys could hear the sound of furious writing, the scratching sounds of a feathered pen scribbling feverishly across the parchment. Sweat breaking on his brow, pains in his chest, the keeper of the keys was forced to stop and catch his breath. The pen kept scribbling across the page, the writer oblivious to the approaching friar. The keeper of the keys gathered his breath, climbed the last few stairs and pushed the door open slightly, peering inside, discovering Thomas Aquinas writing, a large pile of papers scattered at his feet. Thomas Aquinas had returned to the monastery library.

The keeper of the keys heart leapt for joy. Thomas wore a pained expression, he had left the monastery as a boy and returned as a man but the passage had not been easy.

Startled, Thomas dropped his pen. At the sight of his old friend, Thomas leapt from his chair and hugged the keeper of the keys. Thomas broke into tears, the future saint shuddering as he sobbed.

"Now, now lad," The keeper of the keys said, "You must tell me what is the matter."

"I was writing it all down," Thomas said between tears. "My confession." Thomas gathered up his papers. "Almost as soon as I left the monastery, I fell prey to the temptations of wicked sin, I slept with a painted jezebel." And Thomas described the brothel.

The keeper of the keys only smiled, "You know I have often wondered about such things, perhaps even imagined them vividly from time to time. It will not be difficult to forgive you for such transgressions."

"There is more," Thomas said, "I fell under the spell of an alchemical wizard, awed and inspired by his magical knowledge. I have seen things unimaginable and blasphemous." Thomas described the wizard's robot wife and what it felt like performing mechanical surgery on a living machine. The keeper of the keys dropped his jaw in amazement. Thomas explained how he invented the mechanical butterfly and the unexpected moral responsibilities this had brought him. "I could not bring such a mechanical blasphemy inside the monastery and I could not bear to kill it," Thomas said, "So I set it free. I know not where it is now." With a tear streaming down his cheeks he described the death of Albertus Magnus. His voice stammered until uncontrollable sobs wracked his body as he described his kiss and murder of Galatea. The keeper of the keys hugged his dear friend as he confessed. As Thomas described throwing the Philosopher's Stone into the fireplace and the bright white light as the magical powers of the stone transmuted, the keeper of the keys almost wept, such a vision was how he had always imagined God appearing. Thomas told the story of murdering Duke Dracon with clenched fists. "I believe it will not be hard for the Lord to forgive you for that one," the keeper of the keys said. "Some people just need killing."

Thomas described his rescue of the curly haired prostitute from the gallows and his own rescue by the red-headed sisters. There was the frightening pursuit and the unexpected marriage proposal. Thomas finished his story with the suicide of the red-headed sisters.

"Wow." was all the keeper of the keys could say.

Thomas laughed. "I was expecting something a little more spiritual."

The keeper of the keys shook his head in disbelief, "When the bishop sent you out to investigate the world, I don't think either one of us could foresee such events as this. Quite frankly it is a little beyond my religious training."

"I was lucky to come back at all." Thomas said.

"Thank God you did," the keeper of the keys replied. "It is a sign of God's providence."

Thomas felt so confused. "What now," he shrugged.

The keeper of the keys said, "I think we complete our original plan. Now you spend the rest of your life inside the four walls of this library, reading and writing, expanding the wisdom of the church."

Thomas sighed. Once upon a time, burrowing himself forever amongst the stacks of books in the basement of the library had been his dream but now that he had tasted the wider world he was not so certain. He had seen and done such amazing things. Yet, he had also caused such devastating unintended consequences. He had lost control of his passions and committed terrible crimes.

The keeper of the keys hugged Thomas, "You must study like never before."

Thomas did as he was told, reading and writing without stop. Day by day his hair and beard grew longer. The years passed and sometimes Thomas did not see the sun for months at a time. One day, the keeper of the keys passed away as we all must. Feeling blue, Thomas climbed the castle walls and stared at the horizons beyond the monastery library for the first time in a long time. The sun felt warm on his face. The breeze brought him fresh air and new smells. Thomas took a deep breath, hoping to discover that someone, somewhere was baking apple pie. His nostrils searched for the fragrance in vain. A butterfly fluttered towards him, yellow wings gleaming like gold. The butterfly hovered just beyond the parapet walls, dancing on the wind, just beyond Thomas' grasp. It was almost as if the butterfly was taunting him, daring Thomas to jump into the thin air and see if he could fly. Thomas Aquinas returned to the library basement continuing with the solitary studies which would someday make him a saint.

As he descended the stairs, Thomas muttered a prayer for the recently deceased keeper of the keys, begging for forgiveness. There was one secret which Thomas had never confessed to his friend. At the time of their suicide, the red-headed sisters had been pregnant with his children.

In the pastoral countryside there was a curly haired farmer's wife feeding chickens. The chickens gathered at her feet, clucking and scratching, desperate for some of her loving attention and a handful of grain. After escaping the gallows Mary had searched for Thomas, assuming that he was searching for her too. He was not. Thomas wandered, confused and dazed, overwhelmed by events, ending up at the monastery library where he had grown up.

Long after she had given up searching for Thomas - someone found Mary. He was a good man with a strong back, kind smile, and tender hands. He married her and together they raised a family. Surrounded by chickens, children, dogs, and horses, Mary had never been happier.

Then one day a meteor came streaking from the heavens. The fireball roared through the sky, bright enough to outshine the sun. The meteor crashed with a loud smack, shuddering the earth, killing a couple of cows and setting a haystack ablaze. Peasants from miles around gathered to see what had caused all the destruction and discuss what to do about it. The burning piece of space rock sat in the bottom of a deep hole smoldering with an intense bright light which almost seemed holy. Not certain what it was or where it had come from, the peasants were afraid of only one thing - that someday it would leave the earth and return home with the same destructive force it had arrived with. So the peasants bound the meteor with ropes and chains, tying and wrapping the meteor, trying to bind it tight to the earth forever.

The meteor chuckled at these feeble attempts to control it. The Duke had been right about one thing, the Philosopher's Stone would never burn up in a fire no matter how hot. The fire at the alchemist's castle had not consumed it but merely caused the Philosopher's Stone to transmute. The Philosopher's Stone changed from rock to fire, fire to smoke, never losing its true essence. From smoke the magical stone became clouds from clouds to rain, from rain to lightning. As lightning, the Philosopher's Stone did not shoot to earth but into its true home - outer space.

The true reason none of the alchemists were able to recreate the Philosopher's Stone was they insisted on balancing only terrestial elements, earth, air, fire, and water but the Philosopher's Stone was comprised of a fifth element - it was stardust. The Philosopher's Stone was a creature of outer space which had returned to earth again and again to influence the earth and her history. Life itself had been brought to this planet by a meteorite, a piece of a comet's tail crashing into earth. It was a meteorite, a giant plummeting asteroid which had ended the cruel reign of the dinosaurs. Debris from a supernova, crashed into the earth, ended the Ice Age and drove the mammoths to extinction. This caused an insignificant species called man to leave his hunting caves and begin building a civilization. Now the Philosopher's Stone sat in a crater in the European countryside, wrapped in chains which only served to bind its foolish captors. The Philosopher's stone waited.

On a moonless night when no one was awake, not even the wolves, a mechanical butterfly flapped its iron wings. While Thomas Aquinas slept unsoundly, tormented by dreams he did not understand, the butterfly approached the Philosopher's Stone, stuck out its long probing tongue and fed.

www.ingramcontent.com/pod-product-compliance
Lightning Source LLC
LaVergne TN
LVHW012034060526
838201LV00061B/4607